PUFFIN BOOKS

ALLOTMENT LANE SCHOOL AGAIN

Life's never dull at Allotment Lane School, especially for the children in Miss Mee's class. There's Rosemary and Barbara who get Miss Mee in a muddle because they both look the same; Jean who gets lost with her mum and goes home to the wrong house; and Pete who manages to escape eating his liver and potatoes by accident! Then there are special occasions, like the conker-tree planting ceremony and the Pancake Day which turns out very unexpectedly!

Whatever the day, something's bound to happen to the children of Class I. These short, friendly stories are perfect for reading aloud.

Margaret Joy was born on Tyneside. After living for some years on Teesside, where she taught in a sixth-form college and later became a full-time teacher of five-year-olds, she moved to North Wales, where her husband is headmaster of a school for deaf children. They have four children. Margaret Joy has contributed many stories to BBC TV's *Play School* and BBC Radio's *Listen with Mother*.

Margaret Joy

ALLOTMENT
LANE SCHOOL
AGAIN

PUFFIN BOOKS
in association with Faber and Faber

Puffin Books, Penguin Books Ltd, Harmondsworth, Middlesex, England
Viking Penguin Inc., 40 West 23rd Street, New York, New York 10010, U.S.A.
Penguin Books Australia Ltd, Ringwood, Victoria, Australia
Penguin Books Canada Ltd, 2801 John Street, Markham, Ontario, Canada L3R 1B4
Penguin Books (N.Z.) Ltd, 182–190 Wairau Road, Auckland 10, New Zealand

First published by Faber and Faber 1985
Published in Puffin Books 1987

Made and printed in Great Britain by
Richard Clay Ltd, Bungay, Suffolk
Typeset in Sabon

Contents

I
Jeremy the Jerbil

The Christmas holidays were over. Mr Loftus, the caretaker, unlocked the gates of Allotment Lane School again, ready for the new term. Soon there were crowds of children coming up the lane. Some were with friends, some were with big brothers or sisters, some were helping their mothers with pushchairs. Some were just wandering up the lane on their own, having a little think.

Michael was glad to get back to school. He hung up his coat and ran into the classroom. He was carrying a large carrier bag.

"These are for you," he said, dumping the bag on Miss Mee's chair. "They're from my Gran. She says you can have them—she gets fed up with dusting round them."

Miss Mee looked into the bag.

"Christmas cards!" she said. "Thank you, Michael, we'll make something with them."

Then Laura came in.

"I got a Sindy doll for Christmas," she said. "And my Mum says you can have these Christmas cards." She put a bundle on Miss Mee's table.

"Oh, thank you, Laura," said Miss Mee. "They'll come in very useful."

Then the twins came in with their Dad. He was carrying the jerbil cage; the twins had been looking after Jeremy, the class jerbil, through the Christmas holidays.

"Morning, Miss Mee," said the twins' Dad, putting the cage down on a side table. "We've enjoyed having Jeremy very much, but we ran out of sawdust and straw, I'm afraid, so he needs cleaning out."

"Yes, we'll do that today," said Miss Mee. "Thank you very much for looking after him."

"We've brought our old Christmas cards to school too," said Rosemary.

"We took them down yesterday and we don't want them any more," said Barbara, the other twin.

"Great," said Miss Mee. "I'm sure we'll find them useful."

Next, Brenda came in. She was carrying a big carrier bag.

"Guess what I've got for you," she said to Miss Mee.

"Christmas cards?" said Miss Mee. Brenda looked puzzled.

"No, course not," she said. "It's something for Jeremy. It's cardboard rolls. Can I give him one straight away?"

"Yes, all right," said Miss Mee. "He likes one of those to start the day."

They all gathered round and watched. Jeremy sat on his back legs and held the cardboard roll steady with his front paws. He nibbled so fast they couldn't see his teeth—they could only see his nose and whiskers twitching as he bit off little scraps of cardboard.

"He's not eating it," said Michael.

"No, he just likes nibbling," said Laura.

"And he makes a pile of soft scraps to make a den in," said Rosemary.

After lunch everyone had work to do. Some people were cutting the fronts off Christmas cards and making sets of Number Snap cards. Other people were using the backs of the Christmas cards to make shopping lists for their Mums.

Miss Mee was listening to Asif who was reading to her. Pete and Sue were cleaning out Jeremy's cage, while Wendy sat on the floor and held Jeremy on her lap. The classroom was quite quiet, because everyone was busy.

Suddenly—"SNAP!!" shouted Jean and Michael together. Everyone jumped—even Wendy. She let go of Jeremy and he shot off her lap and streaked under the cupboard.

For a moment there was silence, then Pete and Sue shouted:

"Jeremy's gone! He's under the cupboard!"

All the others leapt to their feet, spraying Christmas cards and Snap cards all over the floor. Wendy burst into tears.

"*Sit down*!" said Miss Mee. Everyone sat down.

"And *be quiet*!" said Miss Mee. "We don't want to frighten him."

She tiptoed over to one side of the

cupboard; Jeremy's little grey nose and twitchy whiskers peeped out at the other side.

Miss Mee tiptoed round to Jeremy's side. He disappeared—then peeped out at the other side.

"He thinks I want to play hide and seek," said Miss Mee. She got hold of the long blackboard ruler and pushed it slowly along under the cupboard. Jeremy shot past the ruler and disappeared under the bookcase.

"He's under the bookcase! Under there!" yelled everyone, standing up to see better.

"Put your fingers on your lips, *everyone!*" ordered Miss Mee sternly. "There'll be no playtime, and no hometime, and no bedtime—until Jeremy's back in his cage. We mustn't open the classroom door in case he escapes. So we must stay here, *quiet*— then he might creep out into the open."

She got down on her hands and knees

and slid her hand gently under the bookcase. Jeremy shot out and streaked across the middle of the floor and under the toy-box. Miss Mee picked up the waste-paper basket and gave it to Ian.

"We'll just have to wait," she said.

They all held their breath. It was very quiet. Then Jeremy's twitching nose and bright brown eyes peeped out from under the toy-box. Miss Mee slowly laid one of Brenda's cardboard rolls on the floor near it. Jeremy's whiskers twitched again and he poked his whole head out. He looked at the cardboard roll with his bright eyes. He ran a few steps towards it and sniffed.

Whooosshh! Ian leapt forward.

The upside-down waste-paper basket thudded on to the floor round Jeremy. He was a prisoner at last.

"Hurray!" shouted everyone. "Got him! Good old Ian!"

Miss Mee slid her hand under the basket and caught hold of Jeremy's squirming, furry little body. She popped him down into his cage.

"Phew!" she said. "Thank goodness that's over."

Wendy wiped her eyes and gave a wobbly sort of smile. Pete and Sue put clean bedding in the cage and a pile of cornflakes for Jeremy to eat. Everyone else began to laugh and chatter again. Jeremy sat up and began to clean his whiskers.

"He looks as if he's smiling," said Sue.

"Perhaps he really is," said Ian. "He's glad the holidays are over and he's back in school with us again—I wonder if he'd like a Christmas card to nibble for his nest; we've still got lots left."

2
Paul's Quiet Day

One afternoon Paul was sitting in the kitchen eating his tea. His mother was busy making sandwiches ready for his Dad to take to work on the night shift.

"Miss Mee had a cold today, and she's lost her voice," said Paul, "so we've all been very quiet and good, to help her. And I've worked really hard—Miss Mee said so."

"Good boy," said his mother, wrapping the sandwiches in a piece of silver foil.

"And we listened to some records. One of them was all about instruments."

"That sounds nice," said his Mum, filling a flask with tea.

"I bet I could play a trumpet," said Paul.

"We haven't got one," said his mother.

"We could make one," said Paul. "Look, you've used up all the silver foil. Can I have the cardboard tube in the middle?"

"Yes, here you are," said his mother.

"We've had such a quiet day, I feel like making a great big noise now," said Paul.

"Well, your Dad's still asleep, so don't wake him up," said his mother. "Go and make your great big noise in the street."

So Paul went outside with the long cardboard roll. It made a good trumpet. In fact, Paul thought it was even better than a real trumpet, because he didn't have to move his fingers up and down to make different sounds. He just held it to his mouth and sang into it, and the noise came out much louder at the other end.

Paul marched along, singing all sorts of songs into his trumpet, and now and then shouting into it:

"I'm Paul, I'm *Paul*, mine's the best trumpet of *all*!"

A few doors along from Paul lived his friend, Michael Brown. He had finished his tea and was playing with his toy cars, lining them up on the carpet. When he heard a loud trumpeting outside in the street, he jumped up on the settee to look out of the window. There was Paul, making a lovely noise. Michael jumped down. He was going to go out with Paul—but he hadn't got a trumpet. What instrument could he have? He looked round the room. Then he saw the big, round biscuit tin he kept his cars in. He carefully pushed the lid back down on to the empty tin and raced outside with it.

"Hiya, Paul," he yelled, "I've got a drum."

"Come on then," said Paul.

There was a big red O round his mouth when he had been pressing his trumpet. "Come on then, you can march behind me."

Michael curved one arm round his tin drum and banged on it with the other hand. As he banged, he called out:

"I'm Michael *Brown* with the loudest drum in *town!*"

Further down the same street lived Jean with her mother and her little brother, Sam. It was Sam's bath-time, and he always enjoyed a long play in the bath. Jean liked to kneel on the bath-mat and sail boats with him and squirt him with water to make him laugh. This time she had a plastic bottle with a few drops of washing-up liquid left in it. When she held the bottle under the water and pressed bubbles out of it, Sam laughed. But when it filled up with water and she squirted him with lovely rainbow bubbles, he giggled and gurgled and slapped the foamy water with his hands.

"That's enough splashing for tonight," said Jean's Mum. She lifted Sam out and wrapped a towel round him. "Now you go out to play for a little while, Jean. When Sam's asleep, I'll call you in for bed."

Jean went outside. She was still holding the empty plastic bottle. Suddenly, she heard a peculiar noise, a sort of mixture of trumpeting and banging. It was getting nearer and louder. When Jean saw Paul and Michael, she wanted to join in as well; but she hadn't a trumpet or a drum. She did have a plastic bottle, though. She bent down and picked up a few chips of gravel off the path and pushed them one by one into the top of the bottle. She shook it. It made a lovely "shook-shook" noise.

"Can I come?" she called to the boys.

"You can march behind me," said Michael.

So Jean marched behind the boys. She kept a finger inside the top of the plastic bottle, so the little stones wouldn't jump out. As she shook the bottle up and down and to and fro, she called out:

"I'm *Jean*, I'm *Jean*, I'm the shake-shake *queen*!"

As they marched along, they met someone else from Class 1, Mary Draper. She was running up the road with a loaf of bread under her arm.

"Hiya," called Jean. "You coming?"

"I've got to take the bread home first," said Mary breathlessly. "We didn't have any left for breakfast tomorrow."

She popped inside her house, plonked the bread and the change on to the kitchen table, and rushed out again, still holding the tissue paper the bread had been wrapped in. She caught up with the others and marched behind them.

"We've all got instruments," said Jean.

"So've I," said Mary. She pulled her comb out of her coat pocket. "My Dad showed me how to play this."

She folded the bread paper over the comb and moved it to and fro against her mouth. It made a sort of buzzing noise

which sounded very good but tickled her lips. This is what she sang:

"*I'm* Mary Draper and I play the comb and paper!"

Now there were four of them marching along the street and back again, playing their instruments and calling:

"I'm Paul, I'm *Paul*, mine's the best trumpet of *all*!"

"I'm Michael *Brown*, with the loudest drum in *town*!"

"I'm Jean, I'm *Jean*, I'm the shake-shake *queen*!"

"*I'm* Mary Draper and I play the comb and *paper*!"

A few more friends came out to play. They hadn't any instruments, so they marched behind shouting. "Left, right. Left, right. Left, right." Gary's dog began to bark too.

"This is great," shouted Paul. "It's the biggest noise I've ever heard. We've got the best band in the world."

"I bet it's the noisiest," shouted Michael.

"Yes, yes," shouted everyone else—it was *certainly* the noisiest.

3
Miss Mee in a Muddle

In Miss Mee's class were two girls who weren't like any others in the school. They both had brown eyes. They both had long brown hair tied back in bunches. They both had a dimple in their chins. They both had rosy cheeks. They both sucked their thumbs when they got tired. Their voices even sounded the same when they talked.

They lived in the same house with the same Mum and Dad and the same little brother. They had their birthday on the same day, and they even came to school wearing clothes that looked exactly the same. Only one thing was different about them: they each had a different name. One was called Rosemary, the other was called Barbara.

The children in Miss Mee's class

stared on the day that Rosemary and Barbara first started school. They each wore a red dress and white socks and red sandals, and they each had red bobbles on their bunches.

"They're the same," said little Larry.

"They're twins," said Pete.

Rosemary and Barbara soon got used

to coming to school, and they made lots of friends. But they still always played together and even cried if Miss Mee asked Rosemary to sit at one table and Barbara to sit at another.

The other children in the class soon knew which twin was Rosemary and which twin was Barbara. But Miss Mee didn't. Sometimes she would say:

"What a lovely painting, Rosemary— or is it Barbara?"

Or she would say:

"Put your puzzle away now, Barbara—or are you Rosemary?"

The other children always laughed and told Miss Mee which twin was which, but Miss Mee still went on getting muddled up.

Then one day she had a bright idea. She bought two badges and she wrote "Barbara" on one and "Rosemary" on the other. She asked the twins to put them on.

"There!" said Miss Mee, very pleased

at her bright idea. "Now I shan't make any more mistakes. The twin with the Barbara badge is Barbara and the twin with the Rosemary badge is Rosemary. Now we'll know!"

For a few days this worked very well and Miss Mee made no mistakes. But one afternoon when Barbara, Rosemary and Ian were playing in the play-house, Ian suddenly had an idea. He whispered to the twins, and they giggled. They swopped over badges and giggled again. Then they went with Ian to show Miss Mee.

"We've done something you can't guess," said Rosemary.

"What's that then, Barbara?" asked Miss Mee, looking at her badge to see who she was.

"We've played a trick on you," said Barbara.

"What sort of a trick, Rosemary?" asked Miss Mee, looking at her badge to see who she was.

"They're not Barbara and Rosemary," said Ian, "They're Rosemary and Barbara!"

"We've swopped badges," said the twins together, and giggled.

"Oh dear, now I'm in a muddle again," said Miss Mee.

At home-time she told the twins' mother what they had done. Their mother laughed.

"I'll give them different-coloured bobbles for their hair tomorrow," she said. "Red for Rosemary, blue for Barbara—then you'll know which is which."

Miss Mee thought that was a wonderful idea. Next morning she asked the twins to stand in front of the class. She asked the twin with the red bobbles who she was. Everybody answered for her:

"Rosemary, that's Rosemary!"

"So *you* must be Barbara," said Miss Mee to the little girl with blue bobbles. "R for Rosemary and red; B for Barbara and blue. I'll remember that and never get you muddled up again."

This worked very well for quite a long time.

"Goodnight, Rosemary; goodnight, Barbara," called Miss Mee one Friday evening, and she knew she'd got it right.

On Monday morning the twins were a few minutes late.

"Where can they be?" asked Miss Mee. Then the door opened and everyone looked up and said, "Oooh! Look at the twins! Coo—look at them."

There stood the twins in brown shoes and socks, grey skirts and blue blouses—with shining, *short* hair. And no bobbles.

"We had it cut," said one twin.

"We went to the hairdresser's," said the other twin.

"I think it's lovely, Rosemary—or is it Barbara?" said Miss Mee. "Yes, it really suits you, Barbara—or are you Rosemary?"

All the other children laughed and shouted:

"*That* one's Rosemary and *that* one's Barbara!"

But Miss Mee still didn't know which was which or who was who—and she's still trying to sort them out.

4
A Foggy Mix-up

One school morning when Jean woke up, her bedroom seemed somehow strange. She lay in the top bunk and blinked and wondered why everything seemed so different. The bedroom was very quiet and rather dark. Then she heard her mother filling the kettle in the kitchen downstairs, so she knew it was morning.

"Sam," she called down to her baby brother in the bottom bunk. "Sam, are you awake?"

"Yeth," said Sam. He sounded a bit funny, because he was talking and sucking his thumb at the same time. "Wath the matther?"

"Everything's dark and quiet," said Jean. Sam got out of his bunk and padded across to the window. He pulled open a curtain with one hand.

"Ooh, look," he said. "There'th nothing there."

Jean looked out of the window too. Sam was right: there was nothing there. Usually they could see other houses and a tree, but today there was nothing. Outside the window was thick, white nothing.

"Hello, you two," said their mother, coming in. "I thought I heard someone out of bed! Get under the blankets again, Sam, and keep warm. It's very foggy outside."

She went across and pulled back the other curtain.

"The fog's so thick that I can't even see up the garden," she said. "I can't see the washing-line; I can't see your swing; I can't even see Mrs Dibble's garden next door. The fog has hidden everything."

Later on, Jean and Sam got dressed and had their breakfast. Then they all put on their coats and scarves and mittens, and stood ready at the front door. Everything outside looked strange and white and cold.

"We'll have to go slowly," said Jean, "so we don't bump into things."

"Yes," said Sam. "I'm going to hold Mummy's hand, so I don't lose her."

"Then I'll hold her other hand," said Jean, "so she doesn't lose me."

They walked very slowly to the front gate and along the pavement. Jean's mother held her hand tightly.

"I don't want you dropping off the edge of the kerb," she said.

Two big shining yellow eyes came whining along the road towards them.

"It's an animal," said Sam. "A fog animal."

"No, it's not," said Jean. "It's the milkman's van. He's driving very slowly with his headlights on so everyone can see him coming."

Allotment Lane School was just up the

road past their row of houses, so it didn't take them long to get there. When Jean opened the door near Class 1, everything looked bright and warm inside.

"'Bye, Jean!" called Mum and Sam, and Jean waved goodbye to them before going into the classroom. Then they disappeared into the fog again.

It stayed foggy all day. Whenever the children looked out of the windows, all they could see was whiteness.

"The school's all wrapped in cotton wool," said Jean to Miss Mee.

At hometime, Sam and Mum were there to meet Jean again. They went out into the cold white street. Jean and Sam held Mum's hands very tightly. They walked slowly and carefully down the road and back home again. Mum pushed open the gate and they slowly felt their way to the front door.

"I'll just get my key out," said Mum, "then we'll soon be in the warm, drinking a cup of tea."

She put her key in the key hole, but it wouldn't work. She tried to turn the key, first this way, then that way, then this way again. But the key wouldn't turn at all. Jean's fingers were frozen. She jigged up and down while her mother fiddled with the key. Sam was beginning to sniff, the way he usually did just before he started to cry, and their mother blew on her fingers to warm them up. Suddenly, someone inside the house opened the door!

"Hello," said Mrs Dibble. "Who's that trying to open my front door?"

Sam and Jean and their mother all stepped back and stared.

"How did you get inside our house, Mrs Dibble?" asked Jean.

"It's *my* house," said Mrs Dibble. "*You've* come to the wrong house in the fog!"

"Oh dear," said Jean's mother. "I'm so sorry, Mrs Dibble, we must have lost our way, the fog's so thick. We'd better go back to our house next door. What a stupid mistake."

"It doesn't matter a bit," said Mrs Dibble. "You can go home later, but just for now—would you all like to come into the warm for a drink of tea and a toasted tea-cake? I've just put the kettle on. Come on in."

Jean and Sam and their Mum were very pleased to get out of the cold white fog and go into Mrs Dibble's bright living room. Later on, when they had warmed up a little, they all laughed. What a funny, foggy mistake—fancy losing their own front door.

5
Pancake Day Surprises

Miss Mee was looking at the calendar on Class 1's wall.

"It's Shrove Tuesday tomorrow," she said.

"My Mum said it was Pancake Day tomorrow," said Gary.

"Yes," said Miss Mee. "Shrove Tuesday and Pancake Day are the same thing. And because it will be Pancake Day, there'll be some surprises for you tomorrow."

"Pancakes!" said everyone. But Miss Mee put her finger on her lips and wouldn't say another word.

Next day, when the children came into the classroom, they stood and stared at the large cardboard boxes on Miss Mee's table. She let some of the children have a lucky dip.

Brenda lifted out a bag of flour and put it on the table. Nasreen lifted out a box of salt and put it on the table. Imdad lifted out a bag of sugar. Laura got out a bottle of milk. Sue got out a big mixing bowl and a wooden spoon. Ian lifted out a frying pan. Asif carefully lifted out a box of eggs. Mary found a bottle of cooking oil. Michael found some plates. Miss Mee lifted out a small electric stove; it was very heavy.

"There's one thing left," she said to Paul. He reached to the bottom of the last box and lifted out a bag of lemons.

"Now we've got everything we need for our Pancake Day surprises," said Miss Mee. "We're ready to start."

She put on her painting overall while the children arranged their chairs in a big semi-circle to watch.

"First we'll make the batter," said Miss Mee. She poured milk and flour into the mixing bowl, then cracked some eggs into the mixture, and let Barbara sprinkle in some salt. Everyone had a turn at mixing the batter until it was pale yellow.

"Now I'll plug in the stove," said Miss Mee. She had stood it on an old tin tray in the middle of the table. She switched it on and put the frying pan on the electric ring on the top of the stove. Then she poured some oil into the pan. Next she poured in a little batter and made a small round pancake.

"Toss it! Go on, toss it, Miss Mee," called everyone. So she tossed the pancake nearly as high as the classroom ceiling, then let it rest in the pan to cook on the other side. Now it was sizzling and golden brown. Miss Mee put it on a plate and quickly made enough pancakes for everyone to have a big piece. They all squeezed lemon juice on to their piece of pancake, then sprinkled sugar over it, and ran outside to eat it at playtime.

"I'll just cook one more big one to

share among all the teachers," said Miss Mee to herself, and poured the last of the batter into the smoking frying pan.

A boy from the top class put his head round the door.

"Please can you go to Mrs Hubb about the dinner money, Miss Mee? She says it's important."

"Oh dear—did I add it up wrong?" wondered Miss Mee. She hurried next door to Mrs Hubb's office, and they looked at the dinner register together. Suddenly Mrs Hubb began to sniff.

"I can smell burning," she said. She sniffed again.

"Yes, something's certainly burning," she said. She opened her door and looked into the corridor.

"Oh, it smells very strongly of burning out here," she said. "What on earth can it be?"

Miss Mee suddenly said "Ohh!" and raced back to her classroom. She knew what was burning. But Mrs Hubb didn't—and she was worried. She pressed her finger on the fire alarm bell, and kept pressing. The noise was so loud it hurt your ears.

All the children were outside already because it was playtime, but the teachers had to leave the staff-room and hurry outside to their classes. The children knew that if the fire alarm went off, they all had to line up, so the teachers could make sure everyone was there. Nobody had to be left inside the building if there was a fire.

"Is everyone here?" asked Mr Gill, the headmaster. The teachers all nodded— all the children were there.

"But Miss Mee's not here," said Mary. Everyone looked over to the school. Miss Mee came hurrying out of the door and went over to Mr Gill. No one could hear what she said to him, but they saw him shake his head and say "Tch, tch, tch," to Miss Mee. Then all the classes went back into school one by one.

Class 1's room was full of a horrid smell of burning that made the children wrinkle up their noses. In the waste paper basket was Miss Mee's frying pan, burnt and black, with knobbly bits of shiny black burnt pancake mixture sticking to it. Miss Mee opened all the windows.

"Oh, aren't you going to make us any more pancakes?" asked Larry.

Miss Mee shook her head.

"We could still make lemonade with the sugar and the lemons," said Rosemary. "Couldn't we, Miss Mee?"

"And you couldn't burn lemonade," said Wendy.

"That would be another Pancake Day surprise," said Gary.

"I think we've had enough surprises for one day," said Miss Mee. "Let's do some nice ordinary number work, Class 1."

6
Dinner-time

"Now we're all tidied up for the morning," said Miss Mee, "let's say our grace before dinner. Put your hands together and shut your eyes."

They all put their hands together and most people shut their eyes. "Pete's not got his eyes shut," said Sue.

"Sue's not got her eyes shut," said Pete.

"*Every*body shut their eyes," said Miss Mee. She waited ... then she said, "Now we'll say: Thank you Father God for all our good food. Thank you for our school dinner. We'll eat it all up—"

"—Except the liver," said Pete.

"Even the liver," said Miss Mee. "Amen."

"Amen," said everyone except Pete.

They went along to the dining room.

All the other children in the school were already eating their dinner; Miss Mee's class were last today. The dinner ladies were there, waiting to help them. Everyone picked up a plastic tray and put a knife, fork and spoon in the middle part of it, and a glass in the round part at the end. Then they had to go past all the kitchen ladies at the kitchen counter and say what they would like.

"There's just liver left today," said one kitchen lady, and she gave everyone a helping. There were carrots and turnips and mashed potato. Then there was ice-cream, or banana split, or rice and raspberry juice, or a big cream doughnut. Little Larry couldn't see over the top of the kitchen counter, so Miss Mee had to lift him up to see what there was to choose. Because Miss Mee's class had to wait for the last turn, they were all hungry. The liver had lovely thick gravy, and the mashed potato was soft and fluffy. Everyone started to eat.

45

Pete thought he would start with his doughnut today. It was full of jam and cream. He took a bite and the cream squished out at the sides, so he licked all round the edge, then took another bite. Then he licked the squished cream again and took another bite, then another lick and another bite, turning the doughnut round and round all the time. His doughnut was getting smaller and smaller until there was only one bite left and he popped that into his mouth. It was difficult to chew, as his mouth was very full and his cheeks were very fat. Pete looked a bit like a fat little hamster, with cream all round his mouth and sugar on the tip of his nose.

"Come on, Pete, start your liver and potato," said Miss Mee. Pete's mouth was too full to answer, but he rolled his eyes at Miss Mee to show that he'd heard her. His glass was still empty, so he picked up the metal water jug. As it was rather heavy, Pete had to use both hands. And both his hands were covered in doughnut cream. The jug slipped. Sssperrr-lassssshh!

Pete's glass was suddenly brimful of water—and so was his dinner tray. His potato and liver and vegetables were all swimming in water. Sue waved her ice-creamy spoon in the air. "Pete's spilt his water," she shouted to Mrs Doran, the dinner lady. Paul pointed with his knife.

"There's a puddle all over the table," he called. Pete finished swallowing his doughnut, then pushed his chair back. "It's dripping down on to my knees," he complained.

"Oh dear," said Mrs Doran, and fetched a cloth. Everyone stopped eating and watched as she wiped him down, then wiped up the puddle on the table, then picked up his tray. It was the tray in which Pete's dinner was swimming.

"I'm sorry, Pete," she said. "I'll have to take away your tray."

"Doesn't matter," said Pete, smiling. He was glad she was taking the liver away.

"Of course it matters," said Mrs Doran. "A big boy like you needs to keep his strength up. I'll soon fetch you another great big helping of liver. Just you sit down again, I shan't be a minute."

Pete's smile disappeared. The last thing he wanted was another great big helping of liver. Then Mrs Doran came back with a clean tray.

"There you are, Pete," she said. "Just you get that inside you."

She put the tray down in front of Pete and he looked sideways at it. Then he looked again. On the tray was a huge sugary doughnut, bursting with jam and cream.

"I'm sorry, Pete," said Mrs Doran. "There wasn't a scrap of liver left. I hope you don't mind having another doughnut instead . . .?"

Pete's eyes gleamed as he looked at the huge sugary doughnut.

"No, no, I don't mind at all," he said.

7
Mr Gill Makes a Wish

Mr Gill was busy in his office. He was sitting behind his big desk, thinking about Allotment Lane School and all the jobs that needed to be done.

First of all there was the hole in the roof. Every time it rained, the Big Boys and Girls in the top class had to put buckets and cloths on the floor to catch the drops that dripped down through the ceiling on to the floor of their classroom.

And today the sky looked *very* dark and cloudy. Mr Gill felt sure the rain would soon come pouring down—on to the roof, then in through the ceiling, then drip, drip, drip on to the floor. Oh dear! He sneezed a very loud sneeze.

"And another thing that's bothering me," thought Mr Gill to himself, "is the dinner trays. Some of the children seem to be butterfingers these days. They stand in the line for dinners, chatting to their friends and forgetting that they're holding their plastic tray ready for dinner. Then—C-R-A-S-H! Everyone jumps and looks round—another tray is broken, or at least cracked. Then I have to order more new trays."

Mr Gill sneezed two very loud sneezes, then looked at the pile of letters on his desk.

"Have I got to answer all these?" he groaned. He was talking to himself, and it was a silly question, because he knew he had to, just as he knew that later on he had to talk to Mr Loftus the caretaker about the broken window in the kitchen; someone had kicked a football through it by mistake.

Then he knew he had to phone the school photographer who was coming to take photographs of the children. After that, Mr Loftus was going to show him two broken chairs—so that would mean ordering two new ones. Then one of the children's mothers was coming to see him because her little boy wasn't getting on with his reading, and she wanted to find out why. After that, one of the fathers was coming to see him because he thought there was too much fighting in the playground. Miss Mee was coming to see him to ask for some money to buy new books for the school library; then Mrs Owthwaite's children were going to show him how well they were getting on with their number work. And Mr Gill knew that some children in Class 3 had promised to come and show him the big fat toad they had found on the school field. Later on, when Mrs Hubb, the school secretary, had counted all the dinner money, he would have to drive with it to the bank.

Mr Gill thought it all sounded like a *very* busy morning.

"Oh dear, oh dear!" he said, and sneezed three very loud sneezes, so that his eyes watered and the walls shook. In the next room Mrs Hubb put her hands over her ears.

"And I think I've got a cold coming too," said Mr Gill to himself. He blew his nose very noisily and looked out of the window: it was pouring with rain.

"Oh no," said poor Mr Gill, "not rain! That's the limit, the absolute limit! Just for today, I wish ... I wish that everyone in the school would *disappear* and leave me alone!"

He sat for five minutes holding his aching head in his hands. He sighed and sneezed four very loud sneezes, then started to read his pile of letters.

"There," he said, half an hour later and much more cheerful. "I've read all those letters. I'll just go and ask Mrs Hubb if she'll type the answers to them."

He went next door into her tiny *office*—but *she* wasn't there. "That's funny," thought Mr Gill. "Never mind,

53

I'll go and see if the rain's come through the ceiling in the top class."

He walked along to the classroom and noticed a damp patch on the ceiling, but there wasn't a pool of water on the floor, so this made him even more cheerful.

"But where are the children?" he suddenly wondered. There was no sign of the children or their teacher. Everything was strangely quiet.

"That's very odd indeed," thought Mr Gill, feeling a little less cheerful after all. "I'd better go and look in all the other classrooms."

He did. He looked into every single room, and every single room was *completely* empty. There wasn't another person to be seen. Everything was absolutely silent.

"Oh my goodness," said Mr Gill. "What was it I said earlier? I wish that everyone in the school would *disappear and leave me alone*." And now they have! My wish has come true. I've lost everyone in the school! Oh dear, oh dear, oh dear!"

And he sneezed five extremely loud sneezes.

"What shall I tell Mr Hubb has happened to his wife? What shall I tell the teachers' husbands and wives? How can I tell all the mothers and fathers that their children have disappeared? Oh dear, oh dear!''

Mr Gill's head was aching so much that he thought he'd better go outside for some fresh air. He looked out of the window. The rain had stopped and the sun had come out. He stepped out of the school door and into the playground—and stood still.

There, in the middle of the playground was Mrs Hubb, *and* all the children from all the classes, *and* all their teachers. Mr Gill suddenly felt very relieved that he hadn't made them all disappear with his silly wish.

''*There* you all are, thank goodness,'' he said, but nobody heard him—they were all looking up at the sky. Mr Gill shaded his eyes against the bright sunshine.

''What is it?'' he asked.

''A rainbow,'' said Mrs Hubb. ''Isn't it

beautiful? Look—it stretches right across the sky, right over Allotment Lane School. All the teachers wanted to bring the children outside to see such a beautiful rainbow, and so I thought I'd come out too."

She looked at Mr Gill and said, "But we didn't disturb you, because we knew you were very busy—I hope you didn't think we'd disappeared, did you?"

"Um ... er ... no, no, of course not. Of course not," said Mr. Gill quickly. "But I'm glad I've seen the rainbow. It's made me feel quite cheerful again. Even my cold feels a little better."

He smiled at everyone. Then he gave one more sneeze—just a little one this time—and went back to his room.

8
Anyone Can Make Mistakes

Miss Mee was collecting the dinner money. Most people had given it to her already.

"Gary, have you brought yours?" she asked.

Gary felt in his pockets and searched in his tray, then looked in his jacket pockets. He shook his head slowly at Miss Mee.

"I think I've forgotten it," he said.

"I'm glad I don't forget things," said Paul.

"Anyone can make mistakes," said Miss Mee.

Later, at playtime, most of the children had some sort of snack to take outside. Gary had an apple, Brenda had crisps, Nasreen had a little cake.

"You coming, Asif?" called Michael. "We've got our footy cards."

"I'm looking for my sweets," said Asif. He was searching through all the pockets of his anorak. Then he lifted up all the other coats on the hooks, hunting underneath them for his sweets, but he couldn't see them.

"I think I've lost them," he said crossly.

"I'm glad I don't lose things," said Paul.

"Anyone can make mistakes," said Miss Mee.

After play some people wrote in their diaries. Larry wanted to write about his lovely new bed, but he wasn't quite sure how to write "bed".

"Practise it on the blackboard," said Miss Mee, "and we'll see if you've got it right."

Larry thought for a moment, then wrote "deb" in big white letters on the blackboard.

"It's back-to-front," said Mary.

"Try again," said Miss Mee. "Draw the back of the bed first, then the pillow, that makes *b*. Now put the *e* to sleep in the middle. Then draw a cushion for its feet and a tall end of the bed: that's *d*. Good boy—now you've written *b e d*."

"I think at first I was a bit muddled," said Larry.

"I'm glad I don't get muddled," said Paul.

After dinner it was games afternoon, everybody's favourite. Miss Mee and the girls played rounders, while Mr Gill took the boys out to play football. They had already changed into their shirts and shorts when he arrived.

"Got your boots on?" he asked. "Good—then, let's get out on the field."

First they warmed up, running round the pitch and doing exercises to loosen them up. Then they practised dribbling the ball, first with the easy foot, then with the foot that didn't really want to.

Then they practised different sorts of kicks: forwards, backwards and sideways. After that they chose partners and tried to get the ball away from one another by dodging and pretending and pulling at the ball with their feet. It was all very hard work, and when Mr Gill blew the whistle, they were glad to sink on to the grass for a few minutes' rest.

After that Mr Gill divided them into two teams and they had a really good game of football. In the end the team with the white vests won. Everyone streamed back indoors, breathless and sweating.

"Ten minutes until hometime," said Mr Gill. "I want you changed and back in your classroom with Miss Mee when the bell goes."

They all changed as quickly as they could, talking non-stop as they did so. They packed their football kit into their games bags and went back to class, one by one.

"Come on, Paul," said Mr Gill. "You're going to be the last."

"I *am* ready," protested Paul. "I just can't find my shorts. I've looked everywhere here in the cloakroom. They've just gone."

"Then someone else must have put them with their games kit by mistake," suggested Mr Gill. "Go back and tell Miss Mee; she'll sort it out."

Paul went back to class still looking puzzled. He explained why he'd taken so long.

"You'd better all empty out your games kit," said Miss Mee.

They all groaned and emptied their bags on to the tables. The bell rang and the girls went home, but Miss Mee and the boys were still searching for Paul's shorts. They weren't mixed up with anyone else's games kit. They seemed to have disappeared completely.

"Now think back," said Miss Mee to Paul. "You had them on for football—

where did you put them after you'd changed?"

"I've forgotten," said Paul.

"They must be *some*where," said Miss Mee.

"I've lost them," said Paul. He was beginning to look really upset. "I took off my games shirt and put on my grey shirt, then I took off my football boots and socks and pulled on my trousers..."

His face suddenly lit up and he undid the belt of his trousers. There, underneath, were his games shorts *still on him!* Everyone laughed and groaned.

"I must have got muddled," said Paul.

"Thought you never got muddled," said Larry.

"Well—anyone can make mistakes," said Paul.

9
Operation Panda

Larry and the twins were doing a jigsaw puzzle on their table.

"I can't find the piece for the panda's ear," said Barbara. "We've done all the rest."

The twins searched under their chairs and under the table, but they couldn't find the missing piece. Then Rosemary looked at Larry, who was just standing watching them and smiling.

"You've hidden it!" said Rosemary.

"Give it back, Larry Butler," said Barbara, "or I'm telling Miss Mee."

Larry picked the piece up off the floor and dropped it on the table.

"It was an accident," he said. "It fell under my foot."

Rosemary patted the last piece of the jigsaw into place.

"There," she said. "Isn't he a lovely

panda, all black and white and cuddly?"

"He's very fat," said Barbara.

"That's because he's a giant panda," said Larry.

"Our panda's not fat," said Barbara. She went and fetched the playhouse panda, and they all looked at him. He had been nursed and cuddled and put to bed by so many children that he was long and thin, and even had a hole in his middle where some of the cotton-wool stuffing was coming out.

"Let's show Miss Mee where he's got a hole in his tummy," said Larry.

"Miss Mee, Miss Mee," they called out, going across to her. "Look at Panda, he's losing his stuffing."

Just then a lady came into the classroom. Everyone stopped what they were doing and looked up.

"Why's she got a white coat on?" said Larry.

"Hello, Nurse," said Miss Mee.

"Hello, Miss Mee, hello everyone,"

said Nurse. "Can you come and talk to me, one by one? Then I can see if your hair is clean and shining."

She sat down in the big chair. Pete went straight across to her.

"My hair's lovely and clean," he said. "I washed it under the water in the bath last week."

"I kneel on the bathroom stool to wash mine," said Ian.

"Mine's clean," said Nasreen.

"So's mine," said Mary.

All the boys and girls went up to Nurse and let her look at their hair. Each time she looked and nodded and smiled. Then she turned to Miss Mee.

"All your children have beautifully clean hair," she said. "I think I've seen everyone now."

"What about you, Larry?" asked Miss Mee. "Have you seen Nurse?"

"Don't want to," said Larry, frowning and holding Panda tightly round the middle.

"Just let me look at your hair," said Nurse.

"No," said Larry, holding Panda even more tightly and backing away.

Miss Mee said, "Just before you came in, Nurse, we were looking at Panda. He's grown very thin and he's losing his stuffing, poor old thing."

"Oh dear," said Nurse. "Well, I'm sure I can soon fix that."

She bent over and picked up her bag. She took out of it a fat roll of fluffy white cotton wool and a needle with a long length of white thread in it. She put them on the table next to the jigsaw.

"There," said Nurse. "Now we're ready. We'll do a little operation on Panda."

"What's an operation?" asked Asif.

"We'll make Panda go to sleep, and while he's asleep we'll make him better. You can all gather round and watch. Now, Larry, put Panda flat on the table."

Larry slowly laid Panda flat on his back on the table. Nurse whispered to Panda:

"Now you're going to sleep, Panda, and you won't feel a thing. When you wake up, your operation will be all over."

She held Panda's paw for a moment, then she whispered to everyone:

"Panda's asleep now."

Everyone had gathered round the operating table to watch. Nurse picked up the roll of cotton wool and pulled some pieces off it. She began to push the pieces into the hole in Panda's middle.

"Pull me off some more pieces, please, Larry," she said, and Larry began to pull piece after piece of white cotton wool off the roll. Every time he handed her a piece, Nurse pushed it into the hole in Panda's tummy. Everyone could see that he was already much fatter.

"Nearly finished," said Nurse. "There's just room for about three more pieces ... there! They're all inside him. Now, Larry—needle and thread, please."

Larry picked up the needle and handed it to the Nurse.

"Hold Panda steady," she whispered to Larry.

"He's still asleep," Larry whispered back.

"Good," said Nurse. "Now I'm going to sew up the hole in his tummy, very carefully, with these little stitches—do you see? They won't show at all later on, when his white fur is brushed over them."

She sewed with tiny, neat stitches, then finished off carefully.

"There," she said. "The operation's over. Now you can slowly wake him up."

Larry gently shook Panda, then lifted him off the table. Everyone looked at Panda; his big black eyes gleamed at them all. Instead of being long and thin,

Panda was now big and fat, a black and white, roly-poly panda, just like the one in the jigsaw picture. Larry held him tightly under one arm. Nurse went and sat down again. Then Larry picked up the cotton wool and the needle and put them on Nurse's lap.

"How about that hair then, Larry?" she asked.

"Oh, all right, you can look," said

Larry. He lowered his head so she could see his hair. "I bet it's dead clean, isn't it?"

"You're right," said Nurse. "It is, dead clean."

"Do you do lots of operations in school?" he asked.

Nurse shook her head.

"Oh no," she said. "Panda's was the first I've ever done."

10
Shoes and Shoots

"Why are you walking so slowly, Gary?" asked Miss Mee one afternoon. "Have you got a blister?" She went a little closer and looked at his shoes. "Gary, where are your shoe-laces?" she asked.

"He took them out," said Sue.

"For his conkers," said Mary.

"He wanted conker strings," said Barbara. "We saw him—and Paul, and Michael, and Imdad, and *all* the boys." Miss Mee went round and looked at all the boys' feet. They all had shoes with no laces in.

"Let me see what's in your pockets," she said. All the boys fished in their pockets and brought out big shiny brown conkers. They were all threaded on to shoe-laces.

"Good grief!" exclaimed Miss Mee. "What will all your mothers say when they see what you've done with your laces? You'd better all get off home now." The boys stuffed their strings of conkers back in their pockets and slowly shuffled out. They weren't able to race home as they usually did, because if they had tried to race, their shoes would have fallen off. So they could only shuffle.

The next day Miss Mee took the children across the school field to where the big chestnut tree waved its leafy arms in the wind. "Cor, look right up there," said Michael. They all stood for a minute and looked up, up, up to the very top of the tree. "It makes patterns on the sky," said Michael.

Miss Mee let everyone hunt around underneath the huge tree, until every single conker was picked up and put into a box she was holding. Later on, a Big Boy came and helped Miss Mee to make a hole through each conker. Through each hole they pushed a piece of string (not a shoe-lace), and in the end there were enough conkers on strings for every boy and girl in the class to have one. But before they went home, Miss Mee said, "Look what *I* found under the chestnut tree."

"Uegh," said Paul. "It's just a dirty old conker."

"It's got something sticking out of it," said Michael. "A white bit."

"It's growing," said Brenda.

"Yes," said Miss Mee. "That's its root. If it was planted somewhere, it would grow."

"There's a plant pot under the sink," said Mary, who liked tidying up and always knew where everything was. She fetched the pot and everyone looked at it and said it would be just right for the little chestnut root.

"Can I go and get some soil?" asked Gary. He knew what was best for making things grow, because he helped his Dad on the allotment. Miss Mee let him go outside with the plant pot and a spade from the sand tray. He went outside (but he didn't shuffle this time—his mother had put new laces in his shoes). He was soon back with the pot full of dark brown soil.

"There was a worm, but I made him stay behind," said Gary.

"Very sensible," said Miss Mee. "He'd rather be in the ground, I'm sure."

Everyone watched as Miss Mee made a hole and put the dirty old conker down in the hole, with its little white root pointing downward. All the boys helped to put soil on top of it and pat it down, so that it would feel safe and warm. All the girls tipped a few drops of water on to the soil, so that it would have plenty to drink.

"It won't grow quickly," warned Miss Mee. "We'll have to be patient and wait. It takes a long time for a chestnut tree to grow—even a tiny one."

The children did have to wait and wait. But at last, one day, a little shoot could just be seen poking up through the dark brown soil.

They waited again, and slowly the little shoot turned green, and two very small, bright green leaves uncurled themselves. "It's like a baby tree," said Sue.

"It'll get too big for the pot soon," said Gary. "We'll have to transplant it."

"What a good idea," said Miss Mee. "Yes, it needs to be outside, like a real tree. We must plant it in the ground."

"Like the Princess of Wales did on television," said Rosemary. "She had a spade and she planted a tree."

"But the Princess of Wales doesn't come here," said Gary.

"Mr Gill could do it," said Nasreen.

"Perhaps he could," said Miss Mee.

Wendy and Asif went to Mr Gill's room and asked him if he'd like to be like the Princess of Wales and plant a tree.

"Great!" said Mr Gill. "That's something I've always wanted to do."

So everyone went out into the sunshine, and then Mr Gill came out too. Gary gave him the spade from the sandpit and Mary held the pot with the baby chestnut tree. Mr Gill made a hole in the soil not far from their classroom window.

"You'll be able to look out and see how your tree is growing," he said. He turned the pot upside down and the little baby tree fell out on to his hand; there was still a ball of soil round its roots. Mr Gill carefully lowered the little tree down into the hole and pressed the soil flat and firm all round it. Barbara handed him a jug of water and he watered the little plant. Then he stood up straight again. Everyone was quiet for a moment, just looking at the little tree. Then, suddenly, they all clapped and clapped, smiling at one another.

"It'll grow and grow," said Imdad. "Then we'll have our own conker tree one day."

"Yes, one day," said Mr Gill.

"We'll have conkers dropping down just in front of our classroom," said Ian.

"It'll shade our classroom, so we don't get too hot in summer," said Mary.

"We'll be able to sit under it and sing," said Rosemary.

"Can we sing now?" asked little Larry.

"Yes!" said everyone. "Let's sing about the spreading chestnut tree—you know, Miss Mee."

"Yes, I know," said Miss Mee. "Are you ready, then?"

They all stood in the sunshine and sang. Then they laughed and clapped again, then they all went indoors. The baby chestnut tree stood up firmly in the dark brown soil and waved its two leafy arms in the sunshine.

11
The Mysterious Box

"Miss Mee, Miss Mee, there's a great big box in the playground!" called Gary as he came into the classroom one morning.

"Yes, it's just near the gate," said Asif.

"It's bigger than me," said Pete.

"And me," said Laura.

"It's bigger than Miss Mee even," said Mary. They stood on tiptoe and stretched their fingers up as high as they could, to show Miss Mee what a huge box it was.

"Goodness," said Miss Mee. "Let's go out and have a look at this great big mysterious box."

So Miss Mee and everyone in Class 1 went across the playground and gathered round the giant box. It was made of painted wood, and it had small wheels underneath it.

"I can hear something," said Imdad.

"Ssshh..." He was standing sideways next to the box, with one ear pressed against its side. Everyone stopped talking and went up beside the box and put an ear to it like Imdad. They all held their breath for a moment as they listened.

"I can hear bumping."

"And I can hear swishing."

"And I can hear whooshing."

"And the box is moving!"

It was true—the mysterious box was bouncing up and down, just a little, on its wheels.

"O-oh!" gasped everyone, and backed away.

"Let's go back inside," said Rosemary.

"Yes, let's," said Barbara, her twin, pulling her by the hand. When they were all back inside the classroom and the door was shut, everyone gasped and took deep breaths. They were very glad to be safe inside again.

"Perhaps it was a giant," said little Larry.

"Or a dragon, shut in," said Paul.

"Or tigers fighting," said Ian.

Just then there was a knock on the door and Constable Trim looked in. Everyone looked up at Constable Trim and smiled. They all knew him. He was the policeman they sometimes met walking up Allotment Lane. Once he had come into their classroom and shown them all the different parts of his uniform. He had let Wendy try on his helmet, and her head had nearly disappeared inside. He had let Paul and Michael look at his handcuffs—and somehow they got locked together and had to stay like that until Constable Trim took the handcuffs off at playtime. Now he was saying, "Hello, everyone. I'm bringing two friends to see you later. Come out into the playground at eleven o'clock sharp and we'll see you there."

He gave a big wink and shut the classroom door.

At eleven o'clock all Class 1 were waiting in the playground. Then P.C. Trim came round the corner of the school with another policeman.

"Hello again, Class 1," said P.C. Trim. "This is the first of my friends, he's called P.C. Giles. Now he's going to go and fetch my second friend. Just stay quiet and watch."

P.C. Giles walked towards the giant box.

"O-oh, he's going to open it," whispered everyone, staring to see what would happen. Some people were rather nervous and got behind their friends and peeped over their shoulders.

"D'you think it really is fighting tigers?" asked little Larry.

P.C. Giles stepped forward and undid the door at the back of the box. He let down a wooden ramp, walked up it and disappeared inside. Everyone waited.

There was a sudden hush; perhaps the tigers were eating him...

Then P.C. Giles came out of the box smiling—and leading a huge black horse. Clip, clop, clip, clop, clip-clippety, clop. It came down the ramp with an echoing sound. When it saw the children, it snorted and pricked up its ears. P.C. Giles swung himself up on to the saddle and patted the horse's neck.

"This is Horace," he said.

P.C. Giles showed the children how well trained Horace was—how he could walk and trot, walk in circles or walk backwards or sideways. He told the children that all police horses were trained not to get upset by crowds or sudden noise. He asked them to clap their hands and shout as loudly as they could, but even then Horace wasn't at all worried by the noise; he just pricked up his ears a little higher. Then P.C. Giles got Horace to canter past the children. The horse's great hooves made sparks fly out of the hard playground. P.C. Giles brought him to a standstill again and looked round.

"Who'd like a ride?" he asked.

Everyone looked up at the big black horse. It seemed such a long way up on to Horace's back. But it must be exciting sitting up there, high above the playground. Hands shot up into the air.

"Me! Me! I'd like a ride, I would!" shouted everyone.

P.C. Trim bent down and picked up Asif and held him in the air. P.C. Giles caught hold of him and sat him on the saddle in front of him. Asif looked a bit scared, but he gripped Horace's black mane as tightly as he could. Horace walked slowly round the playground and back to the children. Asif's face was one big smile as P.C. Trim helped him down.

Then P.C. Trim picked up Rosemary and helped her up in front of P.C. Giles. They went very slowly round the playground, then the two policemen helped Rosemary to slide to the ground again.

"It was great, great!" she said to all her friends, who wished they could have a turn too. P.C. Giles swung his leg over Horace's back and dismounted.

"Let's give a ride to someone bigger now," he said.

"Right," said P.C. Trim. "Come on, Miss Mee, we'll help you up."

Miss Mee tried to say, "No, not me!"

88

but her voice came out in a funny squeak. Before she knew what was happening, she had one foot in the stirrup and the other leg was swinging over the top of Horace's great back. She clutched the reins as though she would never let go. With P.C. Trim on one side of Horace and P.C. Giles on the other, she rode round the playground while the children cheered and cheered.

After that the two policemen helped Miss Mee down. Class 1 crowded round her. She had a queer sort of look on her face.

"Oh dear, my legs feel quite wobbly," she said.

"Were you scared?" asked Sue.

"Well ... I'm not sure," said Miss Mee. "I think I was a little bit. It was very high up—you all looked so small."

The two policemen led Horace away to his horse box, and the children went back into class again with Miss Mee.

"I liked that P.C. Giles," said Mary.

"I liked Horace, he was great," said Asif.

"I'd still like to see fighting tigers, though," said Larry.

12
Time for Television

Playtime had finished and everyone was back in the classroom. Paul and Michael were puffing and panting and had very red faces, because they'd just had a fight.

"He started it!" said Paul. "He thumped me."

"No, I didn't! He called me a chicken!" said Michael.

"Merciful heaven!" said Miss Mee. She told Paul to sit at one side of her, and Michael to sit at the other side. "You're my two bodyguards," she said. "Now look at the clock, what's the big pointer at?"

"Twelve!" said everybody, except little Larry, who couldn't count past five yet.

"And what's the little pointer at?"

"Eleven," said everybody, except little Larry.

"Good," said Miss Mee. "That means it's eleven o'clock and time for television. Can you line up quietly?" Everybody jumped up and raced to the classroom door in a big squash, so Miss Mee made them all go and sit down again. "Now try again, *quietly*," she said, and everyone did this time.

"Michael, you can go at the front," said Miss Mee.

"Great!" said Michael, and gave Paul a special look because he was going to be in the best place at the front.

"And Paul can be in charge at the back and shut the door behind us all," said Miss Mee. "Then that's fair."

"Great," said Paul, and gave Michael a special look because *he* was going to be in the best place at the back.

They walked out of the classroom into the hall and sat down on the floor, ready for television. Miss Mee switched it on.

The whole class was quiet, waiting for the start of their programme. They could hear some faint music. Suddenly, the picture went all fizzy, then it went all fuzzy. "It's fuzzy, Miss Mee! Miss Mee, it's gone wrong!" said everyone.

"Botheration!" said Miss Mee, and started to twiddle with all the knobs on the television set. She tried to get the picture right, but it just went on getting fizzier and fuzzier. Everyone else was getting rather noisy, and Michael and Paul were shuffling nearer and nearer to each other again.

Miss Mee switched off the television. She *looked* at Paul and *looked* at Michael. Then she said: "I'm sorry, Class 1, we can't watch television. What can we watch?" Everyone was suddenly quiet, thinking.

Then Brenda said, "I can do tap dancing." She stood up and went in front of the television set. She swung her arms and swung her legs and tap, tap, tappity-tap, tap went her feet, so fast you could hardly keep your eyes on them. Her dark curls bounced up and down. Then Brenda gave a great big last tappity-tap, tap, TAP, and curtseyed. Everyone clapped and cheered.

"I can do cartwheels," said Imdad. He stood in front of the television set and threw himself on to his hands, then on to his feet, and rolled round the room making great big wheels with his body. He ended up on his feet in front of them

all again, smiling and panting for breath.
Everyone clapped again and cheered.

"I can put my legs behind my neck,"
said Asif. He stood up and went in front
of the class. Then he sat on the floor and
pulled his legs behind his head one after
the other. He looked as though he were
tied in a knot. He sat there very stiffly
and managed to smile at the class.
Everyone gave him a big clap too.

"I can stand on my head," said Ian. He

95

gave his glasses to Miss Mee to look
after, then he walked in front of the television set and took off his pullover and
put it on the floor. It made a comfortable
pad. He bent down and put his head on
the pad. Then he carefully put his hands
on the floor too and started to lift his feet
and his legs till they were right up in the
air. He was rather wobbly and came
down rather quickly, then he stood up
blinking and smiling. Everyone clapped
and clapped.

"Watch this!" said Sue. She stood in
front of everybody and put her finger in
her mouth. Then she pulled it out from
her cheek: Pop! She did it again: Pop!
Then twice: Pop! Pop! Soon everyone
was trying it and all over the hall you
could hear: Pop! Pop! Pop! Pop! Pop!

Miss Mee stood up. "Anyone else?"
she asked. Michael and Paul both stood
up and went to stand in front of the television set.

"We know a song," said Paul.

"It's a chicken song," said Michael.

"Just the thing for you two," said Miss Mee, and she made sure everyone was quiet. Paul and Michael looked at each other and began to sing:

"Chick - chick - chick - chick - chicken, lay a little egg for me;
Chick - chick - chick - chick - chicken, I want a little egg for tea;
Chick - chick - chick - chick - chicken ..." they went on. They didn't seem to know how the song ended, but after they'd sung it a few times they hadn't any breath left anyway and had to stop.

Everyone clapped and cheered. Michael and Paul stood in front of the class smiling and smiling, with their arms round each other's shoulders. "Great!" said everyone.

"Yes, great!" said Miss Mee. "That was *much* better than television."

13
Mrs Baxter's Birthday

Every morning Brenda waved goodbye to her mother and set off for Allotment Lane School. It wasn't very far, and there was only one road to cross, so she usually went by herself. When she came to the road, she always looked for the Lollipop Lady. She would be standing on the edge of the pavement, watching the traffic and waiting to help the children cross the road.

"Morning," she would say to them every morning. Even if it was raining cats and dogs, or the snow was stinging their faces, she still managed to smile and say, "Morning."

Mrs Baxter wore a black cap and black boots and a long white coat which covered her from her neck to her knees and kept out the cold and the wind. In her hand she always carried her special sign: a large round notice on a pole. Written on the notice in big letters were the words CHILDREN and STOP. It looked just like a giant lollipop on a giant stick. Mrs Baxter held it up high for all the traffic to see, and then the drivers knew that there were children on the pavement waiting to cross the road. The drivers would slow down and stop to let the children cross safely, while Mrs Baxter stood in the middle of the road until they were all across.

Once when it was very cold and there was sparkling white frost on the ground, Brenda asked Mrs Baxter, "Don't you feel cold, standing out here for such a long time?"

Mrs Baxter laughed and said, "I'll tell you a secret. My long white coat is so big that I can put lots of extra clothes on underneath it! Today I've got three woolly jumpers on, a long woolly football scarf tied round my neck, two pairs of tights, and best of all—I'm wearing a pair of my husband's pyjama trousers under *my* trousers. So you see, I'm as snug as a bug in a rug."

One day in summer Brenda set off for school with four envelopes in her hand.

"Morning," smiled the Lollipop Lady. "You've been writing lots of letters."

"Yes, four," said Brenda. "They're invitations to my party. I'm going to give them to four friends in my class. It's going to be my birthday on Thursday."

"Fancy that," said Mrs Baxter. "It's going to be *my* birthday on Friday."

"Oh, the day after mine," said Brenda. "Fancy that."

After school on Thursday, Brenda stood at the edge of the pavement with Mary, Nasreen, Laura and Sue.

"Hello," said Mrs Baxter. "Are you enjoying your birthday?"

"Oh yes," said Brenda, "They gave me a birthday clap in class, and Miss Mee gave me a birthday sweet, and now we're going home for my party."

Mrs Baxter walked into the middle of the road, holding up her giant lollipop sign on its tall pole. The cars and lorries braked and came slowly to a stop. Mrs Baxter nodded at Brenda and her friends and then they knew it was safe to cross over.

They walked across the road in front of her, then waited at the other side to talk to her. She stood next to them on the pavement as the traffic started up again. She felt down deep into one of the pockets of her white coat and pulled out a paper bag. She gave it to Brenda.

"Here's a little present for your party," she smiled. "You see I remembered it was your birthday today."

Brenda peeped inside the paper bag. "Bars of chocolate!" she said. "That's great—we'll share them out at the party. Thank you very much."

Everyone enjoyed the party, and at the

end they each had a turn at blowing out the candles on Brenda's cake. Then her four friends sang Happy Birthday to You, and her dog, Sheba, joined in too and howled miserably. That made them all laugh, so then they finished off their party tea with the bars of chocolate from Mrs Baxter.

When it was time for them to go home, Brenda and her mother walked to their houses with them. When they'd all gone in, Brenda said to her mother:

"Are the shops still open? Can I buy something?"

"What do you want to buy?" asked her mother.

"Something for the Lollipop Lady," said Brenda. "It's her birthday tomorrow."

Brenda's mother gave her some money and they went into the sweet shop together. When they came out, Brenda was holding something in a little paper bag and they were both laughing.

Next morning Brenda set off to school specially early. When she came up to Mrs Baxter, she kept the paper bag hidden behind her back.

"Morning," smiled Mrs Baxter.

"Morning," said Brenda. "Happy birthday."

"Goodness—you remembered it was my birthday the day after yours," said Mrs Baxter. "Fancy that."

"I've got you a present," said Brenda, handing her the little paper bag.

"A present," said Mrs Baxter. "How lovely."

She opened the bag and peeped inside. Then she started to laugh.

"Well I never," she said. "That's the very best present you could have thought of," and she laughed again.

Can you guess why Mrs Baxter thought the present was so funny? I'll tell you why. Because inside the paper bag was—a lollipop.

14
"You're Scared, Michael Brown!"

Michael Brown woke up one day with a wobbly tooth. He'd never had a wobbly tooth before, and he lay in bed and pushed the tooth with his tongue. It rocked to and fro with a funny little sucking noise.

Michael wobbled it gently with his finger; then he wobbled it a bit harder, but that hurt, so he stopped. He got out of bed and looked in the mirror. The tooth was right at the front of his mouth. His other teeth were straight and firm, but the wobbly one was leaning over sideways.

He went to the bathroom to brush his teeth, but he didn't brush up and down, quickly and briskly, as he usually did. This time he dabbed the brush on his teeth, very carefully, so as not to disturb the wobbly one.

"I've got a wobbly tooth," he told his mother as she made him some toast, and he showed her.

"Fine!" she said. "That means there's a big new one under there, pushing the wobbly one out. Perhaps you'd rather not have toast this morning? Perhaps you'd rather have this thick crust? It might wobble the tooth out while you're biting it." Michael shook his head. He didn't really want to wobble it out straight away.

Michael's Dad was working on afternoon shifts, so *he* went to school with Michael for a change. On the way Michael said, "I've got a wobbly tooth, Dad," and he showed him.

"Fine!" said his Dad. "The sooner that's out, the better. Then the big new one underneath can grow up big and straight. Want me to wrap my hanky round it and give it a quick pull?"

Michael shook his head quickly. He didn't really want it out straight away with a quick pull.

Michael dashed into his classroom and zoomed up to Miss Mee. "I've got a wobbly tooth, Miss Mee, look, I've got a wobbly tooth!"

Miss Mee had a good look and said, "It looks *very* loose to me. Would you like me to get hold of it and pull it out?"

She reached over to get some clean tissues from the box on her desk. Michael shook his head quickly—he really didn't want his wobbly tooth to be pulled out all of a sudden.

In the playground at playtime Michael showed his friend Ian the wobbly tooth. Ian had never had a wobbly tooth, and he was very interested.

"How will you get it out?" he asked. "Will you pull it?"

Michael shook his head quickly and

said, "No, I don't think it would be good for it to be pulled."

Nasreen came over to look at his wobbly tooth.

"Have a toffee," she offered. "That might loosen it a bit."

Michael enjoyed sucking the toffee, but the tooth didn't come out.

"You can have a bite of my apple," said Brenda. "That might shift it." The apple was hard and crisp, but the tooth didn't come out.

One of the Big Girls came to look.

"My Dad says when he was little, they used to tie a piece of thread round a wobbly tooth and then tie the other end to the door handle. Then you get someone to slam the door and the tooth gets pulled out."

Michael didn't think that sounded fun at all. But the Big Girl had some thread in her sewing bag. She made a loop and gave it to Michael to put round his tooth. After a while, Michael said:

"It's no good, the thread keeps slipping off."

"You're scared," said Ian. "You're scared to pull it out with a bit of thread!"

"What do you mean, scared?" said Michael. "*You* found a spider at the back of your drawer and you screeched and yelled, 'cause you're scared of spiders, Ian Thomas!"

"No I'm not!" Ian shouted back. "Anyway, I wouldn't be scared to pull out a little wobbly tooth! You're just scared, Michael Brown!"

"Don't you call me scared, Ian Thomas!" shouted Michael, and he pushed Ian in the chest. Ian staggered back. Then he ran at Michael with his fists up and punched him on the mouth.

"Oucchh-aaagh!" shouted Michael. Then he suddenly stopped looking very angry and looked very surprised instead. He felt round his mouth with his tongue and found the wobbly tooth. It was out! He took hold of it between his finger and thumb and showed it to everyone. His friends all crowded round to see. He opened his mouth and showed everyone the space where the wobbly tooth had been.

"There's something in there," said Ian, looking hard. "A little white thing."

"That'll be my new tooth," said Michael. "I thought it might come through today, so I was just going to pull out the old wobbly one myself... But I let you do it for me. Thanks, Ian."